ATLANTA-FULTON PUBLIC LIBRARY

Snow Day

For Julia Richardson
—M. M.

ALADDIN PAPERBACKS
An imprint of Simon & Schuster Children's Publishing Division
1230 Avenue of the Americas, New York, NY 10020
Text copyright © 2007 by Brenda Bowen
Illustrations copyright © 2007 by Mike Gordon
All rights reserved, including the right of reproduction
in whole or in part in any form.
READY-TO-READ, ALADDIN PAPERBACKS, and related logo
are registered trademarks of Simon & Schuster, Inc.
Also available in an Aladdin Library edition.
Designed by Sammy Yuen Jr.
The text of this book was set in Century Schoolbook BT.
Manufactured in the United States of America
First Aladdin Paperbacks edition October 2007
2 4 6 8 10 9 7 5 3 1
Library of Congress Cataloging-in-Publication Data
McNamara, Margaret.
Snow day / written by Margaret McNamara ;
illustrated by Mike Gordon.—1st ed.
p. cm.—(Robin Hill School) (Ready-to-Read)
Summary: Nia loves snow, but when her wish for a snow day
comes true she finds herself missing Robin Hill School.
ISBN-13: 978-1-4169-3493-6 (pbk.) ISBN-10: 1-4169-3493-6 (pbk.)
ISBN-13: 978-1-4169-3492-9 (lib. bdg.) ISBN-10: 1-4169-3492-8 (lib. bdg.)
[1. Snow—Fiction. 2. Schools—Fiction.]
I. Gordon, Mike, ill. II. Title. III. Series.
PZ7.M232518 Sno 2007   [E]—dc 22   2007000491

Snow Day

Written by Margaret McNamara
Illustrated by Mike Gordon

Ready-to-Read
Aladdin Paperbacks
New York   London   Toronto   Sydney

Nia loved snow.

This winter, there was
a lot of snow.
Nia threw snowballs.

She sledded down hills.

She drank hot chocolate.
Snow made her very happy.

One night,
it was snowing hard.
But Nia did not look happy.

"Nia, what is the matter?"
asked Nia's mom.

"We have had lots
of snow," said Nia.
"But we have not
had a snow day."

"No," said Nia's mom.

She gave Nia a hug.

"You cannot have everything."

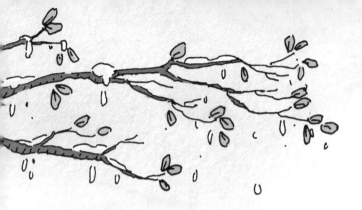

Winter turned into spring.

Flowers grew.

Birds sang.

One Monday in April,
Mrs. Connor looked out the
window.

She opened it wide.
"There is snow in the air,"
she said.

"I do not see any snow,"
said Nia.

"Not yet," said Mrs. Connor.

Later that day,
the sky was dark.
The air was chilly.

Nia woke up the next
morning.

She opened the curtains.
"Snow day!" she shouted.

Nia played in the snow all
that day.

The next day, it was still snowing.

"Snow day," Nia said.

She played
in the snow

until she got cold.

The day after that, snow was
still coming down.
"Snow day," Nia moaned.

"What is the matter, Nia?"
asked her mother.
"I miss school," said Nia.

That day, Nia read a book
with her mother.

She drew a picture.

"I made this a snow day
and a school day," said Nia.

"Pretty cool,"
said her mom.

"Pretty cold!" said Nia,
and they both laughed.

J
E
MCNAMARA   McNamara, Margaret
            Snow Day

R0107830863

FEB 21 2008
MECHANICSVILLE BRAN
Atlanta-Fulton Public Library